READY TO JINGLE

MINA SNOWE

JOSIE MARKS

Content Warning

This book is only for age 18+ readers due to graphic sexual content, including bondage, bullying, multiple partners, age gap, Daddy king, and graphic language. If you are triggered by any of this or are even remotely unsure, please heed this note and refrain from reading this book.

Chapter One
HO, HO, HO!

M erry

"I'm not sure about this, Merry. Who puts an exclusive sex club out in the open like this? It's gotta be full of creeps," my friend Tasha said with a shudder as we got out of the Uber. In front of a place that looked like it might have once been a gym located uncomfortably close to Skid Row in Los Angeles.

Not like me to be in a place like this, but bear with me for a moment. I will explain.

I sighed as I regarded my roommate and best friend's deep frown and pursed lips. Even annoyed, she managed to look dainty and sweet—blond hair tied up in a ponytail, big blue eyes, angelic features. Totally a wolf in sheep's clothing, but what would I do without her? She was loyal, bold, funny, and a certified crackpot. "We're gonna have to see. But we made it all the way here... Maybe we can try?"

Okay, maybe I was the crackpot this time around.

We stood staring at the building for a while. All the windows were blacked out, so at least anyone scrolling by couldn't see inside. People fucking in front of the whole wide world just wouldn't cut it for me unless they were performing on SXTube and I had my trusty ten-speed rabbit with me—but then, what did I really know about sex clubs? Did people still value their privacy when they had their candy canes and nether tinsel exposed for everyone to see?

I heard this place was infamous for its New Year's Eve orgy bash, but I was a get-naked-in-private kind of girl, and that's what I hoped to get tonight.

And I will say this again: the 'I' in this case had to be batshit crazy to even entertain this idea. I truly was desperate.

I rubbed my hands together, having seconds thoughts. I was supposed to be in the library, studying for my last exam before the holidays, but here I was, doing something completely insane—

although I wouldn't say impulsive. I had been thinking about it for months, fantasizing about a sexy holiday present to myself.

Of course, no one except Tasha, the one person who'd seen me at my worst since we first shared a dorm room three years ago, had a clue what I was up to.

No one but she knew I had never done anything like this.

I also had never had an orgasm with a guy, period. Never had anyone make my hoo-ha play Vivaldi's four seasons by angels on harpsicords. And I wouldn't count a climax achieved with my battery-operated BFF—everyone knew it wasn't the same.

Pathetic.

So, I might as well have called myself a fucking virgin, considering that no penis had ever played an Oscar-worthy role in this penis fly trap. No stiff pole had ever made the muff happy. You get my drift. A few robotic strokes—imagine C-3PO awkwardly jerking back and forth, lost in a vast, unknown landscape—doesn't a lover make (sending this PSA to all my exes).

Yep, none of this ass had been kicked, touched, poked, teased, licked by anyone experienced enough to claim a mere quarter-notch in his belt. For the most part, Netflix dates came cheap but the chill part consisted more of a dartboard game where no one had *ever ever ever* hit the bull's eye.

I reckon there's no more doubt at this point about the seriousness of my situation.

Sounds unbelievable, I know. But as I said, I'd never gotten my best jollies.

In short, I was a ball of nerves ready to pop. A complete mess.

My sexual encounters with the few boyfriends I'd gone to third base with had been brief and forgettable. So much so, I tended to avoid dating in general. And the only thing that had ever caressed my ass in a pleasing, satisfying manner was my Victoria's Secret and Fruit of the Loom underwear, depending on my mood.

I had no idea why it had been hard to find someone who could actually get me off and convince me there was nothing wrong with me. That I wasn't just a walking piece of ice with limbs and clothes on. Maybe the boys I'd met in my folks' world had been too afraid of them to truly be themselves with me—it was like asking Little Red's grandma to get her groove on with the wolf, like that would be normal. Yeah, more on that a little later.

Fact was, after meeting too many clueless frogs who seemed to permanently glitch after a clumsy fumble that never got me anywhere near a sliver of anticipation, I decided I had to do something about it. Besides, nobody here knew who I really was—including Tasha—and I wanted it that way.

In truth, I'd made it through almost all of pre-law without sowing one measly wild oat. I could run for office and for once, a candidate's record would be squeaky clean. I'd probably reduce any of my rivals' campaign managers to snotty tears on the election trail.

But you know what I really wanted to do? I wanted to ruin all my chances at an unblemished political career. I wanted to do what any other self-respecting student went to college for: get laid good and proper—with all the off-the-chain sexy bells and whistles—and come screaming like a Valkyrie woman leading her warriors to battle.

Merry, Merry. Might as well live up to my name now.

I looked up at the huge poster hanging on the wall next to the door of the building: "Merry Balls ... Jingle all the way! Come inside and suck your way to Santa's naughty list." Bold as you please.

Merry Balls ... you might say it sounds tacky and ridiculous but I say it had to be a sign and I was supposed to be here.

I looked above the arched doorway at the establishment's name: *TOP D*. Again, I sighed.

"But I see your point, you know," I told Tasha.

Because who in the hell would call their club 'TOP D'? Is it someone's initial? Top Dog? Dick? And in that case, what if the owner had a small pecker? The irony...

Still, I was ready to jump in with my arms, legs, and everything in between. Heart clearly trumped head, for I was ready to walk through those doors and stroll out hours later a changed—blissful—woman.

It was just after six, so the night was at its youngest. A few people had walked inside already. I counted two women and an older guy who looked like a male version of Dame Judi Dench, without the class.

Did I say I was desperate?

Enough to rope Tasha into this craziness. She'd been to a sex club before of course, freaky as she was, so she felt somewhat responsible for me. She made me sick...

I had to nip this in the bud.

"Fine, this sucks, I agree," I continued, "but it's one of these places where no one will know who we are. If we go somewhere else, like that other famous club downtown, Tasters, I dunno, your mother might find out somehow," I warned her. *And other people might recognize me, which would be an entirely other layer of fucked-up.*

Tasha stared at me as though I'd forever lost my ever-loving mind and suddenly sprouted pustules on my face. She clicked her tongue.

"As traditional as she is, Mama would rather burn a Bible than go to a sex club," she stated, and then laughed. "And how on earth would she know we went to a sex club, huh? Or even where the sex clubs are located in this city. She lives in rural Idaho, for God's sake."

I rolled my eyes but couldn't help a laugh, for what she said was true. I'd met the woman once when I joined Tasha on summer break and stayed with her people on the farm. Her mother was the type who would feel compelled to go to confession if she ever accidentally ran a red light. That said, she was a lovely lady who loved her family, and I didn't want Tasha to get in trouble because of me. I didn't have anyone to shock—my mom had passed years ago after a long battle with cancer, and my dad ... well ... he was gone too, but that was another story.

So back to what I said about my family. I was somehow glad Tasha didn't know much about them or the fact my father used to be the head of a Maltese mafia family in LA. No lie. Admittedly, such a thing as a Maltese mafia family hardly existed in California or elsewhere in this country until Dad had put it on the map. He was pioneering like that. A veritable Elon Musk of the city's underbelly. After his sudden death not too long ago, my stepmother had taken over.

Until now, I'd been afforded some freedom to follow my career aspirations until it was time for me to be married off to some stuffy old boss who couldn't tell a clit from a bullet. Luckily for me, my stepmother believed a woman should be educated and above all, shrewd.

So you see, my friend didn't need to know just how 'different' my upbringing had been—at least for the time being. Miraculously, I'd managed to spend years living low-key, away from the glitz I'd been around all my life. One could afford a small degree of anonymity in a big city inhabited by people from all over the world. Not everyone would have heard of the Camilleri name and what it entailed.

Time, however, was running out, for when I was done with my studies in a few years—something my family begrudgingly tolerated me doing—I'd have to go back into the fold, and I'd risk losing Tasha, who might or might not understand why I kept her in the dark.

So now that you have the picture, you must think me pretty sick, and not in a good way. If you only knew...

So here I was, standing fifty feet from some junk-yard, searching for a clue to the mystery between my legs. This was the time for me to see what all the fuss was about. Bullshit, or truth? I had to find out.

Also, it was painfully embarrassing to be in my position at age twenty-one—a freshman in the orgasm department, and not much better in the down-and-dirty sex department, either. I mean, while other girls giggled at each other's stories about carnal adventures and discussed how often they squirted, I was the one who sat listening, with nothing to contribute. Before you start wondering if I look like one of Cinderella's ugly sisters or am covered in scales or something—just no, okay? Don't go there. Tasha often told me I was pretty, with my dark hair, green eyes, curves and height, and she was a blunt bitch so I had no doubt she wouldn't lie to me.

Tonight didn't have to be difficult. The goal was for me to be with someone who knew his way around a woman's private parts without need of an instruc-tion manual and achieve my first ever orgasm with a man. This is why Merry *Frey*—a fake last name as a nod to one of my favorite Norse goddesses—had reserved a special session with not one, but *two*, studs. Better safe than sorry wasn't just a phrase. Apparently, this deed could be a hundred times better if freaky shit was involved, so I was doubling my chances at a great outcome.

Tasha shifted on her feet, arms crossed, obviously still not quite convinced. I knew she'd cave though. Decked as she was in a schoolgirl skirt and a Santa hat, she was as ready to jingle with some random hot hunk as I was. Only, she didn't book a 'Jingling Trifecta Package Experience' like I had. She'd pretty much wing it, as she did with everything in life. Including her sudden, mid-year, three-hundred-sixty-degree switch from pre-med to a Bachelor's program in Mythology, when she got fed up with her first choice.

I stared at her, wondering if I should have put on a naughty Mrs. Claus costume, but instead I'd gone for a body-hugging short black dress that showed off my curves and long legs.

When I took a hesitant step forward, a tiny voice in my head reminded me who I was, that I was still the daughter of a man who'd been one of the most notorious mobsters in Los Angeles, so I had to be careful. People might be watching me at random times, but I had been careful to cover my tracks. I was usually so well-behaved, and so absent from family drama, they often forgot about me.

Mostly though, I was so done with dating losers—they were everywhere. I had started to wonder if I was cursed.

Suddenly, the door of the club opened, the sound making me jump, and a guy walked outside. About as tall as my five-foot-ten and built like a brick house, he wore a black t-shirt with tattoo sleeves on his arm. I trailed my gaze over his strong jaw, down his wide chest, to his large hands. He had a ruggedly dark, attractive vibe to him that made my pulse quicken and my belly flop. You know, like when you see your favorite hot actor on your favorite streaming service and you feel your vajayjay tingle. Then you need to squeeze your thighs together because you suddenly imagine his sexy butt in full Loki costume lying there between your legs, feasting on the goods, licking around your clit and sucking on the nub like a ravenous beast. *Yeah, you know who I'm thinking about...*

From the symbols this man had tattooed on his neck, I pegged him to be part of the Bulgarian mafia. I didn't really know much about that world. Before he married my stepmother during my middle school years, Father had always told me how this life wasn't for me, but over the years I did pick up a few things about it.

The man put a cigarette into his mouth and lit it. He inhaled deeply, then released the smoke, all the while staring at both of us.

His gaze rested on Tasha for a moment before he shifted it to me, slowly scanning my body, then stopping on my lips while my heart began fluttering uncontrollably inside my chest.

"Are you ladies going in or are you just going to stand there?" he finally asked.

He had a perfect American accent, so he was probably born here. Tasha yanked on my arm, giving me that look again. I tossed my mahogany hair behind me and straightened my back. *Fuck it.*

Besides, I knew my stepmother was already scouring for a potential husband for me. I was my father's eldest and I should have been married to some hot shot family ally long ago. It was surprising I'd held off this long, but each day of borrowed freedom brought me closer to my destiny. Would they even allow me to finish law school before they sold me off to some geezer? And if not, would my new husband let me continue my studies?

The thought made me both sad and pissed off. It wasn't like my stepmother hadn't been fucking her way through the LA male population already, yet for some reason everyone closed an eye because her people were so powerful. Really, thanks to her we could continue living a good life.

Besides, to be honest, I also craved a family of my own. Babies to hold. A stable life. Partying and sleeping around wasn't for me. I wanted more.

"Yes, we are coming in," I said to the stranger.

I grabbed Tasha's hand and proceeded to drag her inside. The guy nodded, smirking, and then opened the door for us. Another huge man built like an even bigger brick house, came outside as we entered and stood there like a statue, hands together in front of him. When the door closed behind us, he was chatting with guy number one.

Soon, we found ourselves in a large open space. The red lights and Christmas music were a bit of a distraction, but after a tough year, everyone wanted to get into the holiday spirit again.

"Welcome to "Top D," a fake-boobed, fake-smiling hostess dressed in a Mrs. Claus costume welcomed us by the stairs. I was suddenly glad I hadn't opted for that getup. I wanted to laugh when I read her name tag: Candy. Could this have been any more cliché? "We have a naughty elf strip show that starts in about an hour and if you would like to watch it then please let me know as soon as possible. Are you ladies looking for a male or female companion tonight?"

"Neither for me. I like to do my own hunting. For her now..." Tasha hitched a thumb at me, "you gotta ask her."

I kicked her in the shin for I was already uncomfortable as it is. She didn't have to announce our plans to the whole fucking block. Sweat tickled my brow as I spoke in as low a tone as I could muster, and still have her hear me.

"Er ... I reserved the 'Jingling Trifecta Package Experience' for two men and maybe one who could ... possibly watch us." I quickly rubbed on my belly, which now felt like a warzone.

"Name?"

I coughed into my hand. "Merry," I said, wondering now if my real name was common enough. "Merry ... Frey," I stated my assumed last name. Better safe than sorry—I had to protect myself, just in case. "I said I'd pay in cash." I handed her the exact amount and she thanked me. Oh boy. This was really happening.

"I see your details here," she said sweetly, reading through my booking page where I'd explained about my 'problem.' Heat rose to my face as everything was becoming very, very real. "Hmmm ... okay. You explained well what you wish to get from the experience, and our job here at Top D is to make your fantasies come true." She grinned way too hard and my stomach roiled. *Oh boy, oh boy, oh boy.* "Go and have a seat at the bar and you will be notified as soon as everything's ready for you."

Then she was off, disappearing somewhere down the dark corridor and I took that moment to gather my wits. I convinced myself that this would be way easier and more fun than climbing Mt. Everest in sub-zero conditions, but I wasn't so sure.

Tasha snickered and dropped a kiss on my cheek. "You'll be fine," she said, then grabbed my arm and dragged me to the bar.

"Come on, let's get you a drink to loosen you up a little. If you get any more tense, I could snap you like peppermint brittle," Tasha coaxed me.

"All right, but please let's be a little discreet. I don't want to attract more attention than necessary. I just need to get in some room, do the deed, get off and get out. That's it."

"...Leaving me here alone with all the sharks."

I snorted. "As if. I'm more worried about everyone else in here with you around, roaming the place."

"Nah. I'll just sit here at the bar. How long is it gonna take you, anyway?"

I bit on my lip, no idea what to expect.

"Oh, okay," she added. "Just for fuck's sake don't start talking about nerdy shit on law and history if you want to blend in. All you have to do is be someone else for a minute, get outside of yourself. Not that there's anything wrong with the real you, but this is different. Just relax! You'll be fine!" She jiggled my arm and affectionately flicked my chin with her forefinger.

"Okay," I said as we sat down. We were the only two women in this area. I wondered where that guy with the two women had gone off to. This place had to be huge with private rooms and even a massive orgy room in the back, according to what I'd read. The barman smiled at us. He looked quite in his element wearing nothing but red shorts and a Santa hat. He was handsome, clean and nice looking, but not my type. Probably gay, too. "Can we have two vodkas with orange, please," Tasha ordered. "Make both double."

"Coming right up," he said, giving Tasha a wink. Her face turned red and I rolled my eyes, wondering if she'd end up banging the bartender by the end of the night. She was such a worldly woman and I couldn't think of a better person to bring with me here. I needed all the encouragement I could get. Oddly enough, despite a bit of nervousness and apprehension, I was more than ready.

Ready to jingle.

I knew I gave people an odd vibe sometimes, especially since I had photographic memory and loved nerdy stuff. I enjoyed living in my own predictable world of facts, textbooks, and various causes, where I had a degree of control. Still, despite what people thought, I could let my hair down like the best of them. Although in these times, being a nerd was the height of badassery, too, so I wore that badge proudly.

Still, tonight, I'd just have fun, for the sake of the Elusive Orgasm with a Sentient Being—that's what I was calling it these days. Only not aloud, or Tasha would hit me upside the head with a pan.

We both had our drinks and I ordered another double round because the first wasn't enough to calm my nerves.

That made me a bit tipsy, so when Candy eventually returned, I inexplicably wanted to hug her.

"Ladies, I hope you're enjoying yourselves." She turned to me. I smiled big at her. "Ms. Frey, your room is prepared so if you will follow me..." Before she started heading back with me in tow, she added, "Will you both be going in together? It wasn't in the booking..."

"Oh, no, no. I'm only here for moral support," Tasha said. "I will just have a looksie right—"

"She's going to find someone out here," I said boldly. "I'll be alone."

"Certainly, Ms. Frey. Let us proceed." Another over-the-top grin made her face look like the Cheshire Cat's.

I looked at Tasha and she gave me a reassuring nod. "Go have fun. I'll be okay out here." She grabbed my hand then leaned over for a hug. "Call me if you need me, is that a deal?"

"Deal," I said, swallowing. "I should be back soon."

"Dammit, girl. Take all the time you need! You earned this. Off you go."

After doing some research late last night, I calculated that normally woman needed an hour to fulfil all her needs in a sex club, but since I had never had a proper orgasm, I didn't know if this applied to me. On the other hand, I wanted to believe it could.

I followed Candy through another long corridor bathed in dim lighting, with doors on each side. Whoever owned the club really enjoyed Mariah Carey as her Christmas album had been playing on repeat since we'd entered. As we walked, we were flanked by large Nutcracker soldier figurines lining the walls, and reindeer shaped decorations trimmed with small LED lights. It could have seemed too much, but it really wasn't. I'd have described it as cute, actually, and rather tasteful, considering we were in one of the underground jizz palaces of LA, as I liked to call them, in a spot bordering one of the dodgiest neighborhoods in the city.

"This way. The guys in there will explain everything to you. Wishing you the best," she said, sounding genuine.

My stomach made a funny jolt, but I kept going until I walked inside a large room with black walls and red furnishings. I mean, there was literally no other color anywhere. Not even a decoration or light fixture on the wall or piece of furniture that wasn't black, and no furnishing or upholstery that wasn't a rich red—in either velvet or damask. This included the black and red Christmas tree and garlands framing the windows covered in heavy curtains.

Everything looked like I might have imagined if I'd thought about it long enough. There was a large bed in the middle that could fit an entire family of giants and some long chains hanging above it that would make the Ghost of Christmas Past green with envy. Several sexual toys, lube, and other accessories sat on a small table nearby. There was also a large black leather sofa facing the bed—currently occupied by two of the hottest men I'd ever seen.

My throat went dry, and I found myself rooted to the spot. This was it.

These two men sat waiting for me. I recognized the one from the outside with his smoldering gaze. Both had familiar features, but the second seemed like the opposite as he was a blond with amber eyes and slightly longer hair. The first, who I'd met, had much darker eyes and hair, cropped close to his head. He gave me one of those intense looks that cut through skin, but his expression remained impassive—a man of a few words, apparently. They were both dressed in a black t-shirt and red pants, matching the room.

Damn, they had this planned to a T, with uniforms and everything.

"It's you," I said, feeling overwhelmed by the alcohol that ran through my system and my nerves. I'd paid a ridiculous fee for this experience, so I hoped I wouldn't blow it. Although money wasn't really an issue, I hated to waste it, and more importantly, I didn't want to have to explain how I'd spent several thousand dollars.

My stepmother would be furious, I was sure. Not because she cared about what I did, but she was banking on me making a good match. When she'd taken charge of the estate and the business, everyone thought she wouldn't be capable enough, but she proved them wrong. She was tough, ruthless sometimes, but she treated me and my little sister well, so I couldn't complain.

Still, I didn't want to find out what she'd do if she learned about my shenanigans. She might see it as a slight, a blemish on my reputation, which might affect her plans for me. My world was not for the faint of heart.

"Hi," I finally found my voice and met their gazes. "I'm Merry Frey. I imagine you read my notes about ... what I'm looking for." The tall, blond one curved his lips in response. "You two look like you could be related?"

"Yes, Merry. This is my brother Emilio and I'm Gregory," he finally introduced himself. "And we're here for you." A lopsided smile exposed a dimple on his left cheek, then he stood from the sofa and walked up to me.

He brushed my hair away from my face and caught my chin between his thumb and forefinger. "Would you like a drink? We have wine, or anything you could possibly want." The meaningful look in his eyes told me that indeed, he—they—did have what I want, thank you very much. He caught a strand of my hair and played with it. "You are so beautiful. This is going to be fun.

And then, taking advantage of my distraction—I mean, Brad Pitt had nothing on this guy—he leaned down and kissed me, his lush, full lips incredibly soft and hard at the same time.

I froze for a moment because what's a woman to do when one of the sexiest men alive walks up to her and shoves his tongue down her throat? Pull back? Mumble a muffled thank you? Jump his bones and hope he's as well-endowed down there as he is out here? I left out the 'slap him' option because hell, I'd sort of asked for this.

I mean, take that movie—'When Harry Met Sally.' Hadn't Harry deserved to be blindsided by his friend Sally's fake loud orgasm in that infamous diner scene?

At least, that character had a point of reference.

Which I did not. But as he pulled me close and I felt his huge hard-on press against my stomach, his muscled arms snake around me, my panties got soaked on the spot and I wanted to scream out loud all right.

Jingle holy amazeballs!

I'll take door number three, please. Bone-jumping it is.

Heat rushed through my toes when his hand cupped my ass cheeks and squeezed. His kiss was sensual and unhurried, exploring, urging me to trail my palms up his chiseled pecs and wrap them around his neck. He brought a hand up leisurely to the underside of my breasts and my nipples peaked from the touch. I moaned against his mouth when his tongue danced around mine. He tasted like mint and bourbon—such an intoxicating mix.

As I started to let go, kissing him back, he pulled away from me. Panting, I stared at him in confusion and considered hanging him over the flaming pit of Hell simply for stopping what he had been doing.

Why? The word hung on the tip of my tongue.

He pressed his forehead to mine, which was strangely comforting. "Don't worry, sweetheart. I'm going to make you come like never before and then it will be my brother's turn. We made a deal to get you off before the evening show."

My lips tingled and felt swollen from the kiss, but after the initial wave of frustration, I felt oddly calm. These two didn't come across as amateurs and surely they were going to take care of me.

That said, although Gregory seemed confident enough, he wasn't the first guy who'd assured me he could. I had been with several and each and every one had failed the test, so I wouldn't get my hopes up too high just yet.

I nodded, my boldness soaring as his hand trailed languorously up my arm. I leaned over to catch Emilio intently staring at us, lounging on the couch with his arm spread across the back. "So ... is it just two of you?" I let the question hang between us.

In the past year and a half, I'd been having these dark and twisted dreams on occasion, of me being fucked by three monsters on a four-poster bed. They were all deformed and ugly, but they had enormous cocks and in all my dreams, I always came out fully satisfied and more alive than ever.

Maybe I wouldn't have three monsters, but I *could* score a couple of guys, right?

"Our father should be here in a moment," Emilio stated with a wink. "He will be watching us." He was now standing behind his brother.

I blinked. "I'm sorry, did you just say your father is going to be here?" I stared at him with my mouth agape.

Emilio didn't have a chance to answer because a moment later, another man entered the room, shutting the door behind him.

He was the tallest of them all and had incredibly muscular arms encased in a black long-sleeved shirt. His dark hair was brushed away from his forehead, the sides dipped in a fetching silver that gave him a look of distinction. His fiery gaze sent an instant fire blazing through my core.

Holy shit fucking amazeballs jingle all the way with reindeers frolicking and bells ringing all around!

He had red pants on and a Santa hat, too.

Cocking his head to the side, I noticed his jaw

twitch. Every movement he made called to me, creating a direct line of communication with my coochie, which was profusely thanking me for bringing this god of a man into its midst. His voice was deep and seasoned, like a good aged cognac.

"You can call me Daddy."

Chapter Two
JINGLE BELLS

I vo

Today hadn't been the best of days, and above all of that, I rarely fucked the clients. That was something my sons liked to do on occasion when business was slow—such as it was around the holidays—and they were bored. I certainly didn't care about entertaining some young girl who'd never had an orgasm.

But tonight, I had to make an exception.

When I'd read Merry Frey's information on the online form, something didn't add up. Who paid that much money in cash? Even men cheating on their wives had a secret card they'd use to pay for the kind of entertainment we offered at Top D.

The girl was beautiful with rich brown hair, tinged with red. She had long legs and wide hips, a curvy body—exactly my type. But I'd had strings of pretty women before.

No, what intrigued me was her story. This hunch I had. What was she hiding? And why hadn't she achieved an orgasm with a man before? Had something happened to her?

Too many questions begging for answers.

So I had Candy run checks on both her and her friend. I had all sorts of connections in this city. Yet, nothing was found on a Merry Frey that matched the woman who walked into the club tonight. What we did find was the info on her friend—Tasha Stewart. She was a student at UCLA, who roomed with a certain Meredith Camilleri.

Meredith ... Merry.

I saw the woman's picture—matched it with the flesh-and-blood version.

When I spotted her at the bar, live and in person, it felt like I'd been hit by an anvil, knocked out cold by her beauty. I knew I had to have her, despite what I'd found out about her. She looked young, but it turned out she hadn't lied about her years and she was legal. Still, my body didn't care that I was over twice her age, in my mid-forties. One look at those green peepers, that lush hair and ample curves, and my cock made the decision for me.

Getting hard for a woman wasn't as common a thing as it once was for me—not since Elena. First, that person would have to hold my interest, and most of the women who came to the club looking for thrills didn't pass muster for me.

We'd had people ask us to recreate all sorts of dark, depraved fantasies. Still, in the few years I'd owned this place, never had someone walked in asking purely for an orgasm.

The simplest of things, yet so important for this Merry girl. She wanted—*needed*—to have the best climax of her life, with a real man. Clearly not any of the unschooled bastards she'd been running with so far, who probably had to consult a map and a dictionary to figure out where and what a clitoris was.

My sons had already bet on who was going to make her come first. The Dobrev men always enjoyed a bit of friendly competition.

The worst part of this equation had to be that I wasn't sure how I felt about this. But it wasn't about me this time.

The client always mattered most.

"Daddy?" she echoed my request, staring at me

with those incredible eyes, assessing and judging. "Are you really their father?"

"Yes, but you don't need to worry about him. He's only going to watch," Gregory interjected with a sardonic grin, "while we take turns. So, get on that bed and take off your panties, sweetheart."

She parted her lips like she wanted to say something, but then held back. A hint of apprehension and hesitation flashed across her face, which was understandable. This was completely unfamiliar territory for her.

I dragged my hand through my hair, weighing the situation, now that I'd been dragged into it. I should have mulled things a little more carefully, using the head on my shoulders rather than the other one, before showing up with my cock and balls primed and ready to go.

First off, I was still digesting the fact I had the daughter of Charles Camilleri right here in my club, about to get it on with me and my boys.

I walked over to the black leather sofa and made myself comfortable there, trying to figure out how to go about this. A moment later, Emilio joined me.

"She's fucking hot," he muttered in my ear. Even my son found her sexy. Although he had no idea who she truly was.

Charles Camilleri had been a highly influential

man in LA, a respected leader in the mob circuit. He'd died in a car crash a few years ago, and his wife ran the business like a tight ship now. Bet she had no idea that one of her late husband's little angels was here now, in his den of iniquity.

I shifted on the sofa, running my hands over my chin. This had the potential of being both dangerous and tricky. What if word got to her family where she'd been? But that didn't mean anything—because I'd only fucked a client a time or two in all these years. Would my sons be in danger?

Nah. If she thought there'd be repercussions, she wouldn't even be here. She knew the stakes, and above all, she had grown in the mafia life. From what I'd read about her, she could handle herself well. And she was smart, too. Somebody worth getting to know...

All of a sudden, I wanted this girl for myself, and this wasn't a good thought. I never got territorial with the patrons.

Emilio and Gregory always competed over pussy, but I was too old for that shit—until I set my eyes on Meredith—*Merry*—Camilleri.

"Come on, sweetheart. What are you going to do? I bet you're all wet for me already," Gregory coaxed, approaching the bed and tapping the mattress with his palm, encouraging her to hop on.

"I changed my mind. I want him to leave us alone," she said, her unflinching gaze on me.

Emilio laughed, but Gregory looked annoyed. They both glanced in my direction, expecting me to leave, but I didn't budge. I stayed put.

"Remember how to address me, princess. If you want me to do something, call me Daddy," I reiterated firmly.

Her face turned beet red, but she also licked her lips, which meant she secretly enjoyed what I was doing.

Kinky...

She sighed and then walked to the bed, giving me a glimpse of her sweet round ass encased in black lace panties as she climbed on it. My cock stiffened. The desire to mark my territory came on strong, making me feel like an inexperienced punk.

Holy fuck...

She shifted on the mattress, her gaze roving, assessing. All I needed was to have her alone ... get close to her, feel her, touch her ... and she would never forget this night.

"Daddy, will you leave us alone please?" she asked, putting on a sweet voice. I stood, but instead of leaving, I approached her, taking my time, savoring the sight. She looked like an angel with creamy skin, bejeweled eyes, and legs that wouldn't quit. What I wouldn't give to have those lips wrapped around my cock...

I'd spent a couple of hours scouring the web for information about her. It wasn't easy, but once I had Candy's leads, I could pull out a couple of interesting things.

Like how she religiously spent one full day a week at a legal defense non-profit, assisting the lawyers with pro bono work for underprivileged people.

How she always volunteered at the soup kitchen, and became a passionate advocate for domestic violence victims.

How she liked to visit the animals at a local SPCA and bring them treats.

How she lived simply at her college, always avoiding the limelight.

A young woman who had everything she could want, yet she enjoyed being a good human, walking the walk, without fanfare.

All things I hated to learn—because they made me want to discover her further.

But tonight, I had a goal. And that was to make her explode until she begged me to stop.

"Good girl. Now take off your panties for your Daddy. Gregory might be skilled, but he's not going to make you come like I would," I said with a smile. If I wanted her to myself, I'd have to play Emilio and

Gregory's game. They always acted like eight-year-old children when they competed over something.

The caged look eased from Merry's face as she seemed to come to a decision. I wasn't sure she was comfortable yet, but she did obey me without saying anything, quickly taking her underwear off. I reached out for the prize and she gave them to me without hesitation. Bringing them to my nose, I smelled the sweet aroma, never taking my eyes off her. Her scent was already driving me insane and I hadn't even touched her yet.

"I'll be the one to make you climax, so don't listen to these fools over here, sweetheart," Gregory quipped, and Emilio snickered.

"Yeah, right," his brother mocked.

"Just get the fuck out of here, you two, because you're getting on my nerves. I'll get her screaming for me in no time." Gregory waved us away with an exaggerated gesture.

My younger son had no clue he wasn't skilled enough to give this girl what she wanted. This, I sensed deep in the pit of my stomach.

"But in the form I filled out, I asked for two men and another to watch us," Merry protested. "Can't you get me someone else as a third?" She didn't look too happy.

I inwardly sighed. I loved my sons but right now,

all I wanted was for them to disappear. I doubted I could make this work without letting them have a go at her first, though. Controlling my desire to blast everyone but her out of the room, I caved.

"I understand, princess," I said, thinking ahead and telling myself that if we did it this way, one after the other, I'd eventually get some alone time with her. "So how about this? We try one at a time at first. The other two will be watching from my office." I pointed to the floor above. "If that doesn't work, we'll go with the original plan—no extra charge of course. How does that sound?"

She bit on her lower lip, making me so hard, I needed to adjust my crotch, but I stood still. Waiting. After a few moments of deliberation, she nodded.

Without a word, I put her panties in my pocket and then motioned to Emilio to follow me.

We left the room and headed to my office on the first floor, where I switched on the main screen that gave us a perfect view of the bed in the black and red room. I knew Gregory wouldn't hurt Merry, but I needed to take all the precautions. I needed to figure out why she couldn't orgasm. Maybe this was more psychological than physical.

It would have been better if she let us stay in the room, but this was the next best thing. It would have also been better if I didn't have to watch my sons touch her first—a ridiculous instinct to possess this girl I couldn't yet understand. She was young and ripe, and she put all my protective instincts on high alert. There was nothing I wanted more than for her to call me Daddy while I was fucking her from behind, but my sons would wonder what was wrong with me, and I had no time for that.

But Emilio's dangerous twinkle in his eyes concerned me...

"Wanna bet Gregory won't make her come?" he said once I sat down on the chair in front of the large monitor.

"He won't make her come and neither will you," I told him, noting she was already spreading her legs for Gregory. I focused on her behavior, her movements, the expressions on her face. Her reactions.

Gregory pulled her down to the edge of the bed. I quickly changed the song to another Christmas tune and adjusted my Santa hat. Even in her situation right now, getting ready to be pleasured by a man, her face had a sweetness to it. Purity—that was the word. The scariest part was that I had this insane urge to mark her so deeply, she'd never—*ever*, for as long as she lived—want to be free my touch. My scent. My hands...

I wanted to ruin her.

"You won't have a chance to get to that pussy, Dad. She only wants us to play with her," Emilio said with utter confidence, putting his hands behind his head and plastering his gaze on the screen in front of him.

"We shall see," I muttered, and left it at that. Why argue? All I could do was bide my time.

"Yeah, you're already wet for me, sweetheart," Gregory said, caressing her stomach and then running his hand over her wetness.

Over the years, I'd invested considerable funds into the club and the black and red room had great acoustics. Maybe the branding was a little over the top, but this establishment gave me another good source of income. Politicians, businessmen, and foreigners visited often, booking for private events, and I was the only one in the city trusted enough to guarantee their confidentiality.

I loved hearing her little whimpers in stereo. I guessed there was something to be said for being a voyeur, just sitting back and taking it all in.

Gregory lay on the bed next to her, hitched up her dress, and started rubbing on her clit. From the way she arched her head backwards, closing her eyes and breathing just a little bit faster, she was enjoying the ministrations.

"That feels good," she told him, so he kept the

pace for a while. She moved her hips a little, but after a while, he changed position and kneeled in front of her. I had no idea why he kept ignoring those delicious breasts, that soft skin with graceful dips and curves. Sure, he was hitting the right spots but he should know—while a woman's largest erogenous zone was her brain, the rest of those delicious trigger points were scattered all over her body. Discovering each and every one of them was an exercise in patience, dedication, and detailed sensual exploration. Maybe he was still too young and mindless to understand.

Gregory wrapped his hands around her thighs and started to lick her neatly trimmed pussy, moving his tongue all the way from her ass to her clit. I couldn't deny, the sight made me squirm in my seat, my cock now painfully rock solid. The call of that sweet looking pussy was too strong to ignore. I slid my hand in my jeans pocket and wrapped my fingers around her lacey underwear, relishing the feel of it. I wanted to immerse myself in her, drown in her. Unload my cum in her.

Gregory was doing a decent job, working out what she enjoyed and what she didn't, asking her to guide him, which was considerate and sensible. Maybe he really would succeed tonight.

"I have to give it to him, he's trying hard but this

girl is not a firecracker. She's like a volcano. She's going to explode just with the right amount of licking and teasing," I said.

Gregory was really going for it, licking and rubbing her clit like his life depended on it.

"What are you now, Dad? An expert in pussies?" Emilio asked, laughing.

"Expert in that one, for sure," I playfully countered.

Emilio was a few years older than his brother, but he was fucking around too much. Gregory, on the other hand, was looking a relationship but had been unlucky in love. When his last girlfriend left him, he'd taken it hard. On the outside looking in, one would think the tight-lipped, less extrovert and older Emilio would be the more mature one, but that wasn't the case. Gregory was still pretty young, but he knew what kind of women he liked spending time with.

As a dominant, Emilio was only interested in sexual kink. He liked bondage and giving pleasure through pain. He was never going to settle down and this wasn't good for the business, because he couldn't control his urges. I often found myself having to clean up his messes. One time, he had broken a girl so badly, she ended up on suicide watch.

"Gregory is having a go and you will have your

chance, too, but I am warning you now, Emilio—be gentle with this girl or you'll have to answer to me. She has no fucking idea that you're a psycho," I ground out. And I meant every word.

"Why are you suddenly so protective of this girl? She's no one," Emilio spat, rubbing his hand over the bulge in his trousers. He had no boundaries. What he did have was a pair of cuffs sticking out of his pocket.

"She's a client, that's who she is. She's also not like one of your tough girls. She's a sensitive one, I can tell, so fucking watch out," I snapped back, seeing that my princess was moaning already.

"That's it. Let it out. Are you going to come for me like the good girl you are?" Gregory urged. He inserted two fingers inside her and she moaned some more, nodding vigorously.

Her body stiffened and she shut her eyes, straining, as he maintained his hard and fast rhythm, licking her clit at the same time. I loved the way she writhed on the bed, whimpering and palming her gorgeous breasts. He kept going for about ten more minutes, doing everything he could so she would finally come. For a moment, I thought she was there, for her moans got more intense and louder.

I had a feeling Gregory wanted to make sure she

would come on her own, without the need for a toy or other accessories, but time was running out.

There was no doubt at this point that she wasn't going to get there and I could see that my son was getting tried.

His arms went a little slack and then he stopped, pulling away. He sat by the side of the bed, taking fast, shallow breaths.

When she quieted, she sat up on her forearms, her expression a mix of bemusement and frustration. Damn, I knew this was going to be a challenge, but I had no idea just how much, until then.

"Just give me a few minutes, sweetheart, all right?"

She muttered something under her breath, but I couldn't make out what it was. But when she let herself fall on the bed, beat and dejected, hair a lovely mess, hands covering her face, she looked so vulnerable. And so perfectly fuckable.

"I think maybe we should take a break..." she finally said.

Gregory's chest rose and fell as he took a deep inhale. His hands trailed to his jeans, hovering at the button. He would want to try again, fuck her and try to make her come that way—he didn't like to give up —but she wanted him to stop. Also, a vaginal orgasm might actually be harder to achieve in many cases, and he knew that. He had worked hard, stretched her well, but he needed to count his losses, walk out, and let somebody else handle it.

In the end, he made the sensible choice.

When he walked out, she sat back up and mumbled some words, talking to herself. She raked her hand through her hair and sighed, looking so lost, then started to reason out loud. "Statistically speaking, I'm less likely to achieve orgasm through penetration. There've been studies about this, so what am I going to do? Where did I read that study? Was it Scientific American?" She squinted her eyes, deep in thought. "Boy I should have stayed at the library and studied a little longer. I'm ready for the final, but I'd have been more productive... Oh, I need to ask Professor Gorman about the internship at the Mack & Taylor firm in the spring... Maybe I should get out of here... none of this is going to work," she kept on and on.

I chuckled. Damn, this girl loved to talk to herself. I wondered if this was a habit. But maybe I was on to something now. I'd already figured out she was a model student, excelling in everything. She was probably overthinking everything, which might as well be the culprit in this case.

Her left brain was in overdrive. I mean, the girl couldn't relax! What had she been thinking when

Gregory was eating her out with all he had in him? A law exam paper? An appointment she had to set up for next week?

Gregory had left, so this meant Emilio was going to get his chance to play with her. After figuring out the issue, I had no doubt he wasn't going to succeed—and that worried me.

Emilio was into some dark and depraved shit and I wasn't comfortable with him being alone with her, even if I was watching from upstairs.

I looked up and realized he was already gone to claim his moment with Merry. I watched him enter the room and stand in front of her naked form. Her eyes widened when he put his hands on his hips and looked down at her.

A knot formed in my stomach, and I couldn't shake it loose. But it was too late—I had to let this shitshow play out.

"Are you ready for another round, pretty bitch?" Emilio said. "I'm not a gentleman like my brother, so buckle up, buttercup."

Chapter Three
IT'S NEARLY CHRISTMAS

M erry

Gregory was good. He brought me all the way to the edge, stroking and licking my clit, then sliding to my pussy. When he started fucking me with his tongue, my whole body ignited.

However, I lost that thrill when he added more fingers inside me. It felt like someone had flipped a switch, and I went from needy and throbbing to aggravated.

Now, his brother was here and he was looking at me like I wasn't even human. A tinge of fear crept up my spine, and I wondered if I was still safe. I had to be—this was a business and I'd purchased a service. They'd been around a while, so they knew how to treat a client.

Still, I had my reservations.

If I had to dig deep, deep down inside me, I'd admit their father was the one who lingered in my thoughts and got my juices flowing. The man was gorgeous, with a tall, powerful frame, and an intense dark gaze that seemed to drill right through to my soul. That knowing stare made all manner of sensual promises, and I believed him. Yes, I couldn't lie to myself—after all, I was a practical person. If anyone could get this feeling of completion out of me, it would be him.

For now though, I had Emilio, the fucker who couldn't smile without looking like a character out of a Stephen King book. That said, he was darkly sexy, and hot, and at this point I didn't want to be too picky. I'd get the one-guy-at-a-time deal. Not exactly the two-fer I'd requested, but in hindsight I believed this was best. Daddy had made a good call.

"I'm going to tear you apart, pussycat." Emilio gave me a dark smile, and I wasn't sure I liked it.

Okay, let me hold off on that good call comment for now...

I closed my eyes and braced myself, feeling like the one who always picked the fortune cookie with the shittiest predictions. Like, 'You will be constipated for a week' or 'Watch out for spiders in your pillowcase.' You know, shit like that, probably written by the disgruntled nephew of the fortune cookie company asshole boss person.

Well, my other cookie, on the other hand—the one between my legs, just to be clear—wasn't cooperating. *Bitch.* She gave me nada. Zilch. No 'find orgasm here' sign or some such. No clue anybody could make heads or tails of, including me.

This might turn out to be a bust. At least I could walk out of here any time I wanted. It's not like I was trapped in this place. I also had Tasha, and I could call her so we'd leave together.

Emilio gripped my leg in a punishing grip, so much I cried out in pain. *What in the fuckety fuck?!* Showing no concern whatsoever, he raised it to one of the chains and cuffs dangling from the ceiling.

But before he could restrain me, the door burst open, and in came the very devil I'd been lusting for.

Daddy himself.

A knight in black and red armor.

The sight had me instantly squeeze my thighs together, for my cookie was indeed pleased to see him. More than when she accompanied me to a Daniel Craig movie, or when I sat with her to watch reruns of Lucifer or that Witcher hottie. Yes, my cookie, hoo-ha, coochie, punani, pussy, muff, whatever I felt like calling it at a given moment had strong opinions. And she was letting me know in no uncertain terms: this guy was THE SHIT.

If the huge bulge in his pants was any indication, he was happy to see me too. I felt like a freak for he was so much older than me, but his body was in so much better shape than that of some twenty-year-olds I knew.

The sickest part though was that calling him Daddy made me so fucking aroused.

There was no redemption for me, but did it matter? He was hot, this was a sex club, and kink was the name of the game. My pussy could weep whenever and for whoever she pleased.

I glanced at Emilio and he gave me a dark smile. Obviously, he had different plans for me than his brother. My mind started racing when Daddy made himself comfortable on the sofa in front of the bed, looking straight at said wet pussy.

This time, I didn't want him to leave and I had this feeling he just wanted to make sure his son wasn't going to do anything silly. Because Emilio came across as the crazy one and somehow my gut decided I felt decidedly less nervous with Daddy around. I did my best to forget the not so very minor detail that the guy about to touch my punani was his son, and also the fact that I was attracted to Daddy Santa more than both of his own offspring.

And on cue, my pussy wept some more. If I kept my eyes on Daddy, everything would be all right.

Emilio dropped my leg and produced a pair of Santa cuffs from his pants pocket. I wanted to laugh, thinking how no one had ever tried to turn me on with Christmas toys. The split image of his father but with shorter hair, he was also very handsome. In the right light, his dark brown eyes took on a rich whiskey tone. The tattoos gave him a dangerous air that likely made some women forget their own language at the sight of him.

"Go on all fours and spread your legs for me. I'm going to make you come. I'm not a wuss like my brother. I can take the challenge," he said.

I still had my black dress on and I was glad he didn't ask me to take it off. I couldn't explain why— but the fact his father was here, watching, assessing made me even more subconscious. And hot for him. Boy was it smoking in here.

The black sofa was close enough to the bed so he could see all my private bits at close range. My wet pussy. My ass. Every good trait and every flaw. Every wave of desire that washed over me. I'd be hard pressed to hide just how much I wanted to do that bone-jumping thing with him. Maybe I should tell them I changed my mind and I only wanted Daddy, but my pride reared its head and I would die before admitting that—not after I'd practically kicked the man out before.

"Get on your knees, bitch," Emilio ordered after cuffing my hands together.

I turned and got on all fours, my dress lifted to my waist to expose my ass. I didn't have time to wallow in my self-consciousness for Emilio slapped my ass hard, drawing a scream from me. And then again on the other cheek. My skin smarted, heat radiating off it, and pleasure-pain riffled to my lady bits.

Walking around the bed, Emilio grabbed me by the cuffs and yanked me up, raising my arms until he slid my restraints into a hook hanging from a chain above the bed. I was now on my knees, which were positioned far apart, arms raised up high.

He pushed my dress up a little further, exposing part of my back. I felt Daddy's gaze burning into it as Emilio trailed a hand down my spine and delivered another searing slap.

"Oh shit!" I cried out, shocked and suddenly filled with anticipation.

I felt him climb on the bed behind me and slip two fingers in my pussy, his arm pressing into my ass as he moved.

"Look at that cunt. It's dripping wet all because of a few slaps. I have no fucking idea how Gregory didn't make you come, but I think you need to be punished. You must be holding back." Retreating his fingers, he pinched my pussy hard.

"Ow!" Why did he do that? But oh, when the pain dulled, it kinda felt so good...

"You need to experience some pain before you get to the pleasure. Maybe then you'll appreciate it more," he said, then his ran his hand over my ass cheeks.

Mariah Carey was singing *All I Want for Christmas is You*, which was kind of fitting, but in that moment, I truly hoped Daddy would get to fuck me soon.

His finger grazed my ass and then moved once more down to my wetness. I moaned when he pushed through the folds and dipped a finger inside me once more, then the second one. His rhythm was a tad too rough but once I adjusted, it felt surprisingly good. I wondered if Daddy was watching—the very thought had me ride that hand, striving to catch a feeling that had been elusive for far too long. All I could think about was that beautiful man while his son penetrated me with his fingers—picturing him fucking me on the bed, against the wall, on the floor... Without ever having experienced it, I just ached for his touch, to feel his warm breath on my skin.

Emilio soon found my clit and started rubbing it gently. I closed my eyes. He might have been right. That slap had woken something inside me and I needed more.

More.

"I can't wait to fuck you until you beg me to stop but first, we need to make sure you're ready for it," he said. Then, I felt something moist spread over my ass cheeks.

"Is that lube?" I asked, my voice horse.

"Shhh, I want you to be quiet now and if you're going to be a bad girl, I will punish you," Emilio growled in my ear, and then slapped me again, harder, and I yelped, a stinging pain wracking me.

A vibrating sound reached my ears and he slid the toy inside me. The rhythm was slow, then faster ... slow, and faster.

"Shit," I gasped.

"What was that? Didn't I tell you not to speak?" he asked, so I quickly shut my mouth.

He kept thrusting that vibrator or whatever toy he was using in and out of my pussy for a little while. Then, he put more lube around my ass, and down towards my pubic area, coating it all with his hand. My hips were shaking with anticipation, because I had no idea what Emilio was planning to do next.

"This will make you squeal," he said, placing the vibrating toy on my clit while his finger caressed my anus. I bit on my lower lip, telling myself that he was only setting me up for failure until the intensity of all these sensations made me pant for air as my whole body shuddered. My pulse was drumming in my ears, Emilio then inserted a finger into my other hole and I shifted on the bed, unsure if I liked that, then at the same time he stuck the dildo inside me.

"So wet down there. Easy, little bitch. Your ass needs some training. You like this." Emilio pushed the dildo farther inside me, slowly, and kept penetrating my anus with his finger.

Holy mother of God...

It was a good place to be suspended in, indulging in the build of my thrumming pulse, the quiver in my thighs, the arousing harshness of the whispered words against the shell of my ear.

When he found a good rhythm, he paused for a moment and slapped me hard, never slowing the pace with the dildo. The pleasure-pain had me lose my breath. I thought I was finally going to come like never before.

Emilio pulled out the dildo and replaced it with his fingers.

"Fuck..." I mumbled, losing myself to a whirlwind of sensation, feeling slick heat on my inner thighs. My orgasm was right there waiting... I was on the edge, ready to explode...

But then, Emilio plunged the dildo into my ass. Deep. Rough, ruthless.

I shrieked in agony when intense pain shot through every nook in my body, radiating from that one violated spot.

Mindless to my predicament, he started rubbing on my clit at the same time. Never once did he pause to see if I was all right.

"Bitch, quit your whining," he growled—sounding aggravated.

I tried to pull away. "Fuck you! It hurts!" Strung up as I was, my wrists bruised, and considering the great discomfort I was in, it was hard to move.

Tears stung my eyes, and all I wanted was to crawl in a corner. I could barely muster a word.

Strong arms came around me, comforting, and slowly, gently the dildo was pulled out of me. A different scent awakened my senses, and just then, I knew—it was Daddy's embrace surrounding me.

"For fuck's sake, this one's is a fucking freak! Any other girl would have come five times already," Emilio snapped—heartless.

Daddy's body stiffened, and I could feel the anger

roll off him as he uncuffed me. Meanwhile, my tears broke free and started to fall. How fucking dared he?

"You ... you're a monster. Stay ... away from me," I said breathlessly, my voice muffled as my face was buried in Daddy's black shirt. I hated how weak I sounded. A strong hand caressed my crown, and soft, soothing words reached my ears.

Emilio had never asked if I wanted anal penetration—which I didn't. He didn't care. How was this man allowed to work here?

But then I wondered as Emilio's father pulled away from me: Was I really that messed up? A freak?

Yes, it had been annoying to be like I was, but I'd never thought much about it until now.

My silver-haired knight laid me down on the bed and pulled the dress down, then kissed me on the temple.

"Hang in there. I'll be back," he said in a voice that broke through the sadness.

I didn't know what's happened after that, but I figured Daddy must have punched his son, because Emilio stumbled and fell with a heavy thump on the floor. I tried to turn around, but that was almost impossible because I was still so sore and achy and humiliated.

Daddy's voice boomed through the room. "I don't care if you're my son—enough is enough! You crossed a line. Now get your shit and get out of my club, and don't come back until you've grown into a real man!"

"Fuck you, *Father*."

"Fuck you! Out of my face, before I tear you limb from limb. And learn some respect, will you?"

I couldn't believe he was kicking out his own son to protect me. Trembling and a little cold, I waited. Maybe coming here had been a bad idea. I needed to somehow muster the strength to get up, clean myself a little, and go back home.

There was nothing for me here.

"Yeah, get me out of the way, huh? That's what you want so you can fuck her yourself. You old fool." Emilio just wouldn't give up. But that was the last I heard of him for a big crash ensued—like the sound of something breaking—and then the door slammed shut.

I exhaled in relief when the room was bathed in silence for a moment.

After a while, I felt part of the mattress sink with the weight of a body sitting on it. Daddy's big arms came around me once again. "Are you okay?"

I nodded. He pulled my hair away from my face, then took my hands and checked my wrists. "Don't worry, Emilio is gone now and won't be back."

I sat up and started rubbing my wrists, leaning

my head on his chest as though it was the most natural thing to do.

He was quiet then, seeming to know what I needed in that moment. I had to take some time to make sense of what had happened. I felt like Waldo —lost and never found.

"I'm sorry, I just didn't think I was ready for that," I said when his fingers found mine. He started to massage my wrists, and even through the surreal moment, something sparked between us when our skin touched.

"Don't you dare apologize. Emilio can't control himself. I had no idea what would have happened if I didn't stop him. I should have known..."

I looked into his brown eyes which were full of concern.

"What's your name?" I asked, shocked that I didn't even know it yet. He'd seen me at my worst— yet I didn't know his given name.

"Ivo," he replied. "And you're Merry."

"Yes," I said. "My full name is Meredith, but all my friends call me Merry." That wasn't a lie, at least. "I like Ivo." And I liked the way his name rolled over my tongue. "You know you look a little silly in that Santa hat."

Well, actually, he looked fucking hot in that hat

and I wanted to rip his shirt off, so I could run my hands over his sculptured chest.

He smiled and his eyes twinkled at the corners.

"Thank you for saving me, Ivo, but I guess this is it. I have to get going. I need to see if my friend is okay. She might be wondering the same."

"And your orgasm?" he asked, sounding serious. "I know Emilio was a jerk, but I promise we're not all like that."

"I know. Gregory's nice."

He smiled with pride. "He's a keeper. Works hard, too. I'm proud of him."

"Thank you again for what you did. Takes a lot of guts to take some stranger's side against your son. I know a lot of powerful people who cover for their children's behavior and that's never a good thing."

He put his arm tighter around me and squeezed a little. "Don't get me wrong. I *have* covered for them on multiple occasions, but I guess there's always a breaking point." He sighed.

I picked at an imaginary piece of lint on his jeans, then his hand covered mine. Amazing how easy it was to let go and be myself with this stranger.

"Can you wait for me here? I will be back in a minute."

"Sure," I said. I guessed I could wait a while

before heading out. Although I felt I had probably overstayed my welcome here.

I had a feeling these people were all part of the Bulgarian mafia and I didn't like Emilio one bit. Those guys had a knack for violence and revenge that trumped even the Italians sometimes. Ivo seemed like an exception, or maybe I was wrong.

I was attracted to him, but perhaps it wasn't meant to be. Plus, I wasn't sure I could go through with it tonight. Too much had happened. The worst part was, who could I tell about it? I could confide in Tasha, but I wasn't up to that. My sister was even more inexperienced than me, so she wouldn't understand. My stepmother—we just didn't have that kind of relationship. I had no one else to turn to.

Ivo made me feel comfortable for the first time in a long time and I knew if I was around him a bit longer, I could simply be myself and let go. I didn't have to prove anything to anyone.

But that was just a dream.

The sound of the door opening and closing cut through my thoughts. "Here you go. Hennessy on the rocks. Works wonders to soothe the nerves." He'd also brought a bowl of potato chips for me, as well as a small bag of sunflower seeds. My stomach rumbled and I realized I hadn't eaten in a while.

"Thank you. That's very kind of you," I said,

taking a sip of the strong drink. The liquid burned its way down my esophagus—just what I needed. As I drank and munched on the snacks, our gazes hooked, and my world spun on its axis.

Age was just a number, because I certainly felt an affinity to this man. He was beautiful and as I had just found out, kind. I set the glass down and smiled.

"So," he said. "I bring news. Your friend is fucking a bouncer in one of the rooms of pain. From what I can gather, she's enjoying herself very much," he stated and I nearly choked on a chip.

"Excuse me? Tasha is fucking your bouncer?" I laughed, remembering how I'd just thought about her worrying about me.

"Shouldn't be long though. They've been in there over an hour."

I nodded.

"I can see you're tired."

I nodded again. I should be going now but I didn't want to. I stared at the floor, so torn about what to do. I was so fucked up. A normal person would have run out of there STAT after what happened with Emilio.

"Listen, Merry." Leaning over to take my hand, he trailed his thumb over my knuckles. Again, his touch was electric. "I know you are thinking about staying here, with me, but Emilio's actions have ruined what was left of a perfectly good experience. I have a proposition," he said, then paused, likely to gauge my response.

"Yes?"

"Why don't you go home with your friend tonight... you need a familiar face to be around for a while. I can see you're much better, too."

My heart sank. Maybe after all the failed attempts at reaching a climax, he also thought me a weirdo.

"But I want you to come back tomorrow, at eight PM sharp."

I turned to face him, lips parted as a question dangled from my lips. He returned my gaze with a fervent one of his own. Firm. Determined. Serious.

He wants me.

"I need you to wear this dress again, and no panties, no bra, and this time, we will be completely alone. The club will be closed tomorrow. I'll send a car to whatever address you give me, and bring you here. Is that clear?"

"Yes, Sir."

"Sir?"

"Daddy. Yes, Daddy."

"That's my girl. Now go on and rest. You'll need it for your big day tomorrow."

Chapter Four
DECK THE HALLS

Ivo

She'd refused my offer of a car picking her up, and showed up here in an Uber. When she arrived, I thought it wise to take her to a different room, this one decorated in green and gold, with hints of red for the holidays. I had a table set up, and I'd brought in take out from the Chinese restaurant.

What mattered was that I had her all to myself. Emilio and Gregory both had their chance and blew it. Couldn't say I was sad about that.

The girl needed to be taken care of and I had to have a bit more time with her. She was so fucking beautiful, inside and out, and in just a short time, I was intrigued by her. I didn't want to let her go without her experiencing something that would change her outlook on life.

An orgasm with a man. *Me.*

A flash image of her sprawled on the bed with her gleaming pussy exposed, legs wide open, entered my mind. Last night, it was the last thing I saw in my mind's eye before stroking myself to a toe-curling orgasm, followed by a deep, long sleep with dreams of a dark-haired, green-eyed temptress.

Merry wanted to experience a first, but so did I. I'd never been into much younger women before, or even considered Daddy kink as a thing. But somehow, just finding out about Meredith Camilleri, I just couldn't help yearning for her. She was a paradox, not like other women in my brutal, unyielding world. The fact her family were rivals of mine, or that she still had no clue who I was, didn't stop me from craving her in the worst way.

I should know better.

Merry put her chopsticks down on her plate and rubbed on her belly. "Oooh, I'm full. Thank you for dinner. It was delicious."

"You're welcome," I said, loving how she'd enjoyed her meal with enthusiasm, digging in. She was an entirely different princess altogether...

"So tell me, how old are you, Ivo?" she asked. "I've been meaning to ask but we didn't have the time."

"Hmm, how old do you think I am, Merry?" I also loved how her name was so fitting for this time of year. Maybe she was my Christmas present, perfect for me to unwrap...

"I do have a good memory, but I'm not too good with the guessing game.Sixty?" Her eyes twinkled like gems.

"Fuck, no," I said, knowing she was pulling my leg. "I'm only forty-five."

"Are you married to Emilio and Gregory's mom? Someone else?" A delicate frown creased her face.

"No. We've been divorced a long time now."

"One more question. Why did you come to the room when Emilio was here? Were you trying to protect me?"

She seemed genuinely interested in the answer, so I'd give it to her straight.

"Well, my son's been known to be a little ... impulsive and hot-headed."

"...And he's the true freak."

I laughed at that. "Can't argue with this reasoning."

She opened her mouth to say something, then seemed to think better of it.

"Tell me what you meant to say," I insisted. I wouldn't let her cower and retreat and fold into herself. I hoped she understood she didn't have to, with me.

"Well ... I wanted to say although what Emilio did was ... too much, I ... I ..."

"Yes? Go on..." I encouraged.

"I liked the tying up and the roughness and ... dunno how to describe it. It's as if ... as if I could let go and be overwhelmed but in a good way. If I feel safe I could ... maybe, you know..."

"Come," was all I said in response.

Picking up both our drinks, I led us to the couch, where we sat comfortably next to each other. I handed her the glass and put my arm around hers. "Look at me."

"Hmmm?" She did as I asked.

Drowning in her eyes, I leaned down, down, down, until my lips found hers and captured them in a demanding kiss. She tasted even better than I imagined. Her lips parted and she didn't hesitate to kiss me back. I deepened the kiss, sliding my tongue into her mouth, and my cock went as hard as a rock. I didn't think it could get any harder. *Shit.* I grabbed a fistful of her hair and pulled her head back.

Her eyes were the color of emeralds, her mouth swollen and pink.

"I'm hungry again. Let your Daddy feast on you."

Before she could say a word, I stood, picked her up, and carried her to the bed. Time for us to play for a little while.

She kissed me again, nipping on my bottom lip and driving me absolutely crazy. I pressed her closer to me, kissing her deeply until our tongues collided. She moaned into my mouth that just about made me lose my self-control.

"Do you trust me, princess?" I asked, hovering above her.

She nodded.

"And from now on, you'll call me Daddy."

"Yes, Daddy," she replied, and I groaned at the sound of that rolling off her lips. I didn't think I could ever get bored of her calling me Daddy.

I pulled a scarf out of my pocket and quickly blindfolded her. Then, after making sure her wrists were healing nicely, and she nodded for me to continue, I put her hands in the cuffs that were built into the bed on each side. Her legs went into regular chains, with a Christmas garland I had weaved into them. She didn't make a sound, just let me restrain her without hesitation. The little festive details were hilarious. I put a lot of thought into pleasuring my princess.

"What are you going to do to me, Daddy?" she

asked, trying to jiggle her arms. She was stuck, unable to move, at my mercy.

"What is the fun inme telling you, Merry?" I then proceeded to rip her dress off her, tearing it apart. My heart hammered in my chest at the sight of such bounty. Full, deliciously round D-cups plopped out like a jack-in-the-box, the nipples stiff and alert. As I'd instructed, she wore no undergarments.

"Why did you do that?" she squeaked. "How am I going to get home now?"

I climbed on top of her and caressed her breasts, with feather-light strokes at first.

"Don't worry, princess. Daddy will take care of you," I assured her, and then took her perfectly round pink nipples into my mouth, stopping for a second when she jolted, inhaling sharply. Those little fools hadn't even touched her beautiful breasts, or paused long enough to appreciate her. They thought that if they licked her for a while, they would win the challenge, but a woman needed and deserved much more than that.

I started squeezing her breasts with both of my hands, their weight filling my palms, then licked her nipples until she was wriggling on the bed, begging me to stop.

"So you like this, huh? I now know one of your weaknesses, princess." I sucked hard on her nipples again, swirling my tongue over them and biting gently.

"Oh, God," she moaned.

"God won't help you now," I said, laughing, then bit her left nipple harder than I anticipated. She cried out, shaking her head, and I pinched the other one, rolling it around my fingers.

"Enough ... stop. Please..."

"Sorry love, I have no intention of doing that. I'm only just getting started."

I didn't require the aid of any toys this time. I just needed to use my imagination to make her lose her goddamn mind. Her hips tensed and she yanked on the chains.

"Are you wet for me? Do you want me to touch you down there, princess?" I asked, pressing my hand over my hard dick. I didn't even remember the last time I'd tied another woman up and fucked her hard. Never had I even had one in Merry's situation, and I had a fair bit of experience in the bedroom.

"Yes please, Daddy. I want to come so badly. Can you stick your cock in me?" she pleaded, falling so easily into the little girl role.

"Oh, darling, of course, but not yet. First you need to come for Daddy like a good little girl." Lowering myself down to her opening, I inhaled the sweet scent of her arousal.

She was already spread, ready, and so, so wet for me. I blew into the sensitive flesh there and she arched her body, ass off the bed, when the cool air hit her.

"Ivo ... fuck..." She pushed her hips downward, trying to get her sweet pussy in my face, searching for my touch. The anticipation of what was coming made me horny as fuck. Placing small kisses over her clit, I then licked it slightly, gently. Her pussy was so engorged and glistening with her juices, and I felt her throbbing for me, pulsating with the need for release.

"Daddy is pleasing you, my princess," I said, and then proceeded to lick her in earnest, because I just couldn't hold off any longer.

She moaned loud as I worked her up to a frenzy, her exquisite sounds echoing in the room. Her opening was wet and slick. I wanted to stick my dick in her, fuck her until she couldn't take it anymore, until I sprayed my cum all over her perfect, luxurious tits. Fuck her hard everywhere in this room... but I needed to be patient in savoring her.

"Oh, Daddy. Daddy, this feels so good," she said, squirming.

I licked, rubbed and caressed her clit. She tasted like a sweet wine, but I couldn't get enough.

I reached up and tweaked both her nipples. The

more stimulation I gave them, the wetter she got for me. Now that I'd found what made her tick, I had to take full advantage. Yes, she loved rough handling, enjoyed the role play, but she also wanted a man who'd give attention to her body the way he was supposed to. Emilio had been too fast, too impulsive and inconsiderate. Merry might find herself gravitating to the world of bondage and submission, but what he'd done—pretty much bulldozed into her ass —just didn't cut it.

I let my tongue taste all of her, spreading her legs to get better access.

She whimpered with a tad more urgency now, but I wasn't planning on letting her come just yet. Rubbing her clit with my fingers, I spread her folds with my tongue, then fucked her with it, in and out.

"So wet, so soaked for your Daddy, but now I need you to stay very still for me," I commanded, pulling out for a moment.

She mumbled something incoherent and I reached out to squeeze her nipple while I continued to tongue-fuck her sweet, tight hole. At that point, she was panting, so I finally inserted my finger inside her, pushing to the back where her G spot was.

My little Merry ... she loved it all, going by her cries of ecstasy. And she was trying really hard not to move, listening to me obediently. She was so fucking wet, so fucking tight—almost like a virgin. The thought that some other fucker had come between her legs before me, that my sons even might have-done the same, made me so furious and mad.

I fingerfucked her and continued to lick the bundle of nerves that was the nub. Merry's pussy was so hot and trembling for me. I could feel it, so I added the second finger. It was a sweet, sweet torture which caused her to push her crotch harder in my face.

"Daddy ... oh, Ivo," she moaned, straining her whole body.

I knew she was close. I kept thrusting my finger in and out of that cunt, picking up my speed while my tongue kept doing all these wonderful things to her clit.

Then, when it was time, I sucked on it like it was a lollipop at the same time, never easing the rhythmic fucking with my fingers. She was coating me with her juices, shouting out her pleasure, and arching her back off the bed.

Yes, baby, yes...

"Fuck, omigod ... what—"

Her voice broke down, sweat covered her magnif-icent breasts, and then, just like that, her dam burst free, and she was coming for me.

And coming.

And coming.

She roared, screaming out my name, yelling intelligible words, cursing, spouting the most beautiful language I'd ever heard. And all the while, I kept thrusting my fingers into her wet cunt and intensifying the sucking on her clit, milking her. Her body finally spasmed with the last remnants of ecstasy, trembling and fully experiencing this release for the first time ever. It was the most beautiful thing I had ever seen.

Fuck, she didn't even realise how hot she looked right then, taking long, deep breaths, and staring at me with wide green eyes.

"Fuck, Ivo ... I think I finally..." Her body trembled violently, and she gasped for air, unable to speak further. Now that spot was so sensitive, but I didn't stop massaging it. I simply slowed down. Her nipples stood erect, and my cock was unbelievably hard. I think my boxers were smeared with pre-cum.

"You were such a good girl for your Daddy. I told you I could make you come, princess." I laughed, so fucking proud of myself.

When our eyes met, she looked pleased and most likely surprised with the intensity of her first ever orgasm. Reaching out to her hands, I quickly released her from the bondage. My blood boiled with excitement and anticipation, because now I'd earned the privilege of fucking her brains out.

She collapsed on the bed, running her hands over her breasts, then over that dripping cunt, exhaling sharply.

After that, I also released her legs.

"How was that, my princess?" I asked, drawing her in my arms. She leaned into my hold.

"Amazing." She shook her head. "I think I'm whole again and I have you, Daddy, to thank for it," she said, stretching out her endless legs on the green and gold sheets. I bought my fingers to my mouth and licked them, tasting her. Then, I put them in her mouth, running my hand over her red lips. She tasted like honey and vanilla.

"Suck on those fingers, princess," I ordered, and she did, like the good girl she was. She sucked all around them, sensually, and my cock was ready to finally be taken care of.

After she licked it all clean, I undid my pants and took off my t-shirt. My boxers came next. When she glanced at my shaft, her jaw dropped and her eyes went wide.

"Good, but you have been a naughty girl, so now I have to punish you," I said, getting off the bed.

I was so horny for this girl, for her mouth and her hands....

She smiled, going on all fours, and then she started crawling on the bed towards me. Perfect—an open invitation to play.

"And how are you going to punish me, Daddy?"

"I'm going to fuck your mouth, kitten."

Chapter Five
ALL I WANT FOR CHRISTMAS IS YOU

Merry

I orgasmed. I *finally* fucking orgasmed. I kicked the beam, blew my lump, cracked the marble ... and it had been the most amazing experience of my life. A million times better than what I expected—and thank goodness I'd asked for three men, not one. If I had come here thinking to just have one, then I might never have met him. I was most likely finally fucking cured.

Ivo was twice my age, but he put a lot of effort into making this happen. He made me feel like I had gone to heaven and back. Plus, he had the stamina of a young man, and could more than keep up with his sons. Matter of fact, he was better.

I couldn't bloody believe it, but I did doubt him for a second when he put the blindfold on me and tied me up.

I was so restricted and somewhat uncomfortable, because I really wanted to see what he was going to do to me. In the end, it was all worth it and he had done many freaky, but wonderful things to me. I was in the literal sense dripping wet for him, for his cock that I hadn't seen yet—but there was nothing I wanted more than to have him inside me.

Now he was standing in front of me with his massive cock out, still wearing that silly Santa hat. His body was a work of art. He must work out a lot to keep that kind of physique. His stomach was ripped and each dip and curve was spectacular.

"I don't think I'm very good at this. I haven't given too many blowjobs before," I told him, feeling a tad embarrassed. His sons were hot; well, this entire thing was disturbing enough ... but Ivo? He was handsome, confident, and highly experienced. And most of all, he acted like he gave a damn.

His face brightened, then his eyes darkened as he stood in front of me with his erection pointed at my face. He was huge, thick, and veiny. I had been with a few boys in the past, but I had never seen such a large cock before. He was my Daddy, and they could not hold a dollar-store, fifty-cent candle to him.

"Oh princess, just start sucking it. Besides, this is not for your pleasure. This is your punishment, so don't look so excited," he said with a mad gleam in his eyes.

I sat on the bed, feeling myself getting wet again, and then wrapped my palm around his girth. Ivo shut his eyes as I licked the tip, unsure if that was what he wanted me to do. He tasted salty and wet as I licked what seemed to be his pre-cum. *Hmmmm* Then, before I couldn't protest, he put his hand around my head and shoved his cock in my mouth.

I struggled with that size, gagging right away, but Ivo didn't even flinch. He fisted his hand in my hair and growled when he forced my head to move.

"That's right, take it all like a good girl. The gagging will stop soon, princess. Relax and let me fuck your mouth," he instructed, staring down at me with fiery eyes. I placed my hands on his thighs as tears rushed to my eyes at the strain of it all, but at this point, I really didn't care how uncomfortable this was going to be. I just wanted to please him, because then he was going to ram his hard cock into me soon enough. My pussy jumped for joy at the thought of it.

He thrust his cock into my mouth, first slow,

then hard and fast, pulling on my hair as he did. It seemed he was getting thicker and bigger as my tongue danced on the tip.

It was a punishment because he didn't give me any control. He was fucking my mouth, groaning out loud when I swirled my tongue around him. He didn't let me use my hands, which frustrated me a little.

Ivo was rough, pulling my hair so hard, I cried with pain. His hips were stiff and the tension around his groin almost visible. For a second, I thought I wasn't going to last as the intensity of his movements burned through my mouth. He sped up, then his cock bumped into the back of my throat.

At the same time, I was drenched with the naked desire and exhilaration of having him inside my mouth.

"Is that nice? Does your pussy like when I'm fucking your mouth so roughly?" he asked. Obviously I couldn't respond for my mouth was stuffed fuller than a trussed Turkey on Thanksgiving. Tears began streaming down my face. "I'm going to come and you'll swallow every drop, Merry. Are you ready to take your Daddy's cum? I know this is uncomfortable, but you have been a bad girl. You need to know your place, kitten."

Fuck, I couldn't take it anymore when he started

to push harder. Everything hurt—my jaw, my throat—but he kept going. I gagged, shaking my head, and a moment later, his whole body strained. The muscle in his jaw ticked, and his cock grew thicker as he slowed down his movements.

"Fuck, *fuck*!" he growled, spraying my mouth with a big load of semen.

This was all new to me. He tasted salty and warm, so I swallowed him quickly, trying to control my gag reflex.

When he finally pulled himself out of my mouth, I felt so used and abused—in a good way. I rolled on the bed, mulling what had just happened. Did I like this? Ivo had purposely made it rough, but maybe if there ever was going to be a next time, then I might be the one in control. I wanted to experience everything.

He wiped my tears away with his hand and then reached out for something.

"I think this could be your little reward," he said, holding his fist in front of me, palm up.

I scrambled off my feet and touched his fingers. He unfurled the fist and on his palm was a miniature Santa hat.

"What's that for?" I asked, my voice horse.

"A hat for my cock," he said, sounding amused.

I just couldn't help laughing. I quickly took the

thing from his palm and kneeled in front of him. His cock was moist and still pretty much hard, so I slid the hat on on the tip.

"Dear lord, it fits," I said.

Ivo glanced down at it and shook his head.

"Look at yourself. You took it all in your mouth and now you get to see me like this, all festive and ready to jingle your pussy," he said, grabbing my chin, and lifting it slightly. "Get back on the bed and spread your legs wide, my princess, because Daddy is ready to fuck you."

He didn't need to tell me twice. Grabbing my hand, he helped me stand up. I couldn't wait to have him inside me.

I lay on the bed, staring at his chest as I waited. I noticed he had some tattoos on his back, but none on the front. Amid some interesting symbols he had inked, I suspected some writing was probably in Bulgarian, or Russian.

"Are you going to fuck me hard?" I asked as he pulled the small Santa hat off his cock and strolled towards the bed, watching me.

My jaw still ached a bit, but that didn't matter in this moment.

"Yes, I am. Are you sure you want my cock messing up your perfect little pussy?" he challenged, getting on the bed and then straight away sucking on my nipples. No one had ever given so much attention to my breasts. Sure, my boyfriends had touched me, but no one had ever taken proper care of them. Ivo almost made me come again with the way he sucked on each of my nipples.

"Yes, please, Daddy," I begged. Every time I called him Daddy, Ivo upped the ante on his teasing, as though I'd won some super difficult battle in a video game and leveled up. He bit on my nipple, stuck his hand between my thighs, and rubbed all around with raw, animalistic fervor. I yelped with pain, for a second ready to slap him when suddenly, he flipped me around.

One minute I was on my back and the next I was lying on my stomach. He grabbed both my hands before lowering himself over me again.

"You need to know one thing, my princess. I don't make love, I fuck hard, so the question is: Are you ready to be fucked hard?"

I nodded enthusiastically. "Yes, Daddy, please fuck me hard. I need you," I said, struggling against him when he pinned me down.

Those three last words seemed to awaken some inner animal. He fisted a hand in my hair and then ran his other hand over my anus. This new sensation wasn't like before, for this time around I wasn't afraid, but full of anticipation.

"You have no idea how much I want to ruin that fine ass," he muttered. "Go up on all fours."

"No, Daddy, you need to fuck me. I'm so wet for you," I disagreed, whimpering that he was taking so long.

In response, he pulled my hair painfully hard, forcing me to lift myself up, and I whimpered with discomfort. Fuck, he hadn't been joking when he said he was rough. Still, I wasn't afraid.

"Are you fucking telling me what to do, Merry?"

My throat went dry.

"I'm sorry, Daddy," I mumbled, suddenly scared that he was never going to give me what I wanted most.

"Good. You should be sorry. I need to stretch all your holes and you're going to love it. Trust me," he said, with those last two words assuring me that I had nothing to worry about.

I had already reached an orgasm earlier on, so I was supposed to be fulfilled, but deep down I knew I wasn't. The man had just unraveled me, tore me up with pleasure, but he didn't fuck me yet and I needed to feel his cock pumping into me. He made me feel whole and right, so much I didn't think I could just walk away, and forget this ever happened.

He let go of my hair and then I arched my hips

upward, so he'd have better access to my pussy and ass.

A mixture of trepidation and excitement warred within me as he gently grazed his fingers around my slit, then to my ass, and back all the way down to my clit. My knees shook when he spread my ass cheeks and licked me there with a skilled stroke.

So good...

He took his sweet time, making me wait for what felt like an eternity.

"Please..." I managed breathlessly.

"Shhh."

Realizing he wasn't going to give me what I wanted right then, I closed my eyes and submitted to the onslaught of pure pleasure.

He stopped licking for a moment, and I whined in protest. "Oh yes, you have no idea how much that turns me on," he said and then stuck two fingers into my anus. Slow and steady. Damn, that was different from yesterday. Exciting. Maddening. "Just relax and breathe."

He fucked me gently at first, rubbing my clit at the same time, with the same rhythm.

Oh God ... oh sweet fuck...

The pressure built so fast, I thought I was going to come from just that touch. I was so ready for him, my juices dripping on his hands.

"Tight ... you're so tight down there, but my cock will fit in," he murmured, shifting on the bed so his cock was nudging my pussy.

"Shit! Yes ... oh Daddy just fuck me. Do it! Please ... Daddy!" I thought I was going out of my mind, the fire in my body now too much to bear.

"Since you say it that way, your wish is my command,," he said, and then he rammed into me, withdrawing his fingers from my backside. He filled me so utterly, so completely, more pressure built up in my core.

"Shit... Oh shit yeah..."

He emitted a deep, guttural groan as he started to move inside me, steady then faster, rougher, his fingers gripping my thighs

"Shit... You feel like heaven."

I coated him with my juices as he hammered his cock into me like he'd promised.

And I took him in—all of him. Every excruciating inch.

It felt unbelievable, amazing.

I gasped. "Harder, Daddy..."

He thrust with more force, satisfying my request.

Then he inserted a finger into my ass once again and I screamed because I really didn't know what was happening to me. My heart jackhammered inside my chest, heat bubbling on my cheeks and neck. His cock moved in my pussy simultaneously with his finger in my ass. I had no words for how this felt.

Better than fantasy.

Better than Carrie finally snagging Mr. Big in Sex and the City.

Better than the Arizona Cardinals winning the NFL championship after the longest drought in history.

Better than ... *chocolate*. There, I said it.

"How do you like it? Does this feel good?" he asked, keeping up the pace.

"Daddy ... oh, fuck. I can't take it anymore," I moaned.

He laughed, but ignored what I said with a, "Yes you can, and you will." The fucker.

My holes were getting a pounding, delivered by the sexiest man alive.

Wasn't I lucky?

He pulled his fingers out, slid his arm under me, and pressed up on my stomach, lifting me off the bed, so my back was flush against him.

"I need to come inside you. To feel you, raw, just like this." His voice strained, he poured those sensual words in my ear. "So tell me, princess, are you on birth control?"

I nodded, not really knowing my own name at this point or if I was even human.

"I'm clean, too. You knew this coming in—no one can fuck or suck if they're not clean."

"So am I, said it the form..." I bit out as he mercilessly massaged my breasts. He smelled like cinnamon and Scotch with a hint of smoke. I'd finally figured out his scent, and I loved it.

"Ivo, *pleeeeeeease*," I begged, feeling a kinship with that meme of a skeleton waiting on a bench. My pussy waved the white flag of surrender, ready to be pillaged and turned inside out.

He thrust and thrust until at motherfucking last, I reached the promised land, floating under a blanket of stars.

I screamed for Daddy, seeing the fireworks as he let out a monstrous roar and released himself into me. Panting and moaning, we both came apart together. The orgasm ricocheted through me with an bang, taking with it everything that I was in that moment and dropping me dead in a pool of melting lava. I cried out his name, over and over, as the tidal wave of heat pulled me under.

Then, bit by bit, I rose back to the surface. My body felt raw and well-used. Ivo laid me down on the pillows, covering us both with the soft green sheets.

"That's my girl. Now let's sleep for a while. You

did good, kitten. Daddy is proud of you," he whispered.

I just wanted to close my eyes for a second to relish this bliss, because he was so good to me and I felt so, so tired all of a sudden. I liked his warmth, and how well he fit around my body.

Soon enough I was drifting away, thinking that this was probably a dream. Only a pleasant dream.

Chapter Six
MERRY AND BRIGHT

Ivo

Merry erupted like a volcano—what a thing of beauty. She came so hard, so freely, so completely— witnessing that was a treat in itself. I was ready to curl up next to her and drift off, too, but that wouldn't be wise. After she fell in a deep slumber, I stayed by her side for a moment, listening to her breathe.

I checked the clock to see it was almost ten PM. It might seem silly but I was concerned how she could sleep so peacefully with a relative stranger, away from her familiar surroundings.

I couldn't leave her here in the green room. Tonight we were closed but Gregory and Emilio had keys and it wouldn't be the first time they showed up with some girl they were fucking or dating. Especially Emilio, since he was such a man-whore. The last thing I wanted was him coming over and finding Merry here, in bed, naked—alone. That wouldn't bode well for her, and I'd never allow her to be put in such a predicament.

After today, I had to give some serious thought to Emilio's future at the club. At this point, he had become something of a liability. But I'd think about that tomorrow. Today was for Merry. Only Merry. My princess. It had been a proper whirlwind since she first came to Top D last night—but from the start, the connection between us couldn't be denied.

Could it lead somewhere? *Dare I even entertain the notion?*

No. I could not.

I slowly got up and lifted her up in my arms. Shegave a little moan, so I went still until I was sure she was still fast asleep. Then, I carried her out of the room, upstairs to my office.

Over the years I had refurbished the club, so now I had a stylish bathroom and a comfortable double bed in my private quarters.

When I had her settled in the sleeping area, I went to my desk and called Candy.

"Yeah, boss," she answered, sounding like she was working through a mouthful of food. Or maybe sucking on some candy cane, which she would never be caught without during her work hours.

Candy came across as a bit of an airhead, but nothing could be farther from the truth. She had been my loyal employee for many years, and we always looked out for each other.

"I want to talk to you about Merry." She knew about tonight. In fact, she'd ordered the takeout meal for us and had it delivered.

"You got it bad for this girl, Ivo. You need to be careful nobody finds out who she is. Good thing you had her in the red room out back all evening yesterday, and tonight nobody's there," she said in a whisper, even though I knew she lived alone with a black cat, and liked it that way.

"Once she wakes up, I'm going to send her home, so don't worry about it," I told her, because that was the plan. A plan I hated because I wanted more of my princess.

"Yeah, right."

He could practically see her smirking.

"Just make sure nobody saw or recognized her yesterday, okay?"

"Whatever you say, *Daddy*. Consider it done." Candy ended the call with a giggle.

I went to sit on the edge of the bed, staring at her, and wondered how on earth I hadn't met her before. Our paths must have crossed at some point in the past and yet, I had no recollection, which meant it likely didn't happen. With a loud sigh, I went to my wardrobe and grabbed some clean clothes to put on. I could still smell her all over me and I wished I would never shower again.

Merry had a hell of an evening today, reaching a milestone in her life, so she needed to get her energy back. I headed to the bathroom to take a quick shower. Once I was dressed and freshened up, I went downstairs to the club to see if everything was in order for tomorrow. I went behind the bar and filled up a glass with water, then downed the whole thing. I had a lot on my mind lately. After I'd broken my engagement with Anika, she wouldn't accept my decision. Her family was powerful enough to create some serious problems for me if I didn't backtrack and marry her like they intended.

Meeting Merry I already knew wasn't just a distraction—but a complication. I just didn't have the headspace to deal with that right now, AND watch my hide at the same time. Turf wars always had a way of breaking out when one least expected them, and Anika's people were notorious for starting some pretty fucked-up shit. What had I been thinking to get involved with her anyway? It had seemed like a good idea at the time. Trouble free...

Now though, if I wanted to avoid an all-out carnage, I'd have to put the marriage proposal back on the table. That's what it would take to appease them, and that's what I would do. Mafia families were like royalty. Marriage was a convenient strategy for cementing alliances. My people depended on this. On me.

Hungry again, I grabbed a bag of peanuts from a bar shelf, and added to that a bag of chips and some Christmas chocolate to take to my princess. For sure, she'd be ravenous when she woke up.

My princess. I really had to stop thinking of her as mine. All we had was one night. One, and no more.

I needed to make sure Emilio and Gregory wouldn't start blabbing about her all over the place. First thing in the morning, I'd call them over and have a chat with them. I couldn't take any chances.

I went back upstairs to get some club admin work done. My lovely volcano girl slept on, during which time I'd finished all the tasks on my plate.

I watched her for a while, like a fucking stalker. I just couldn't help myself. She was additive and most likely the best lay I ever had—which was crazy and a bit ridiculous, too. Especially at my age, and everything I'd done.

If she ever got involved with another man, it was going to take him a while to satisfy her, and he most likely wouldn't unless he was dedicated to pleasuring her. In my experience, most men were selfish bastards.

I couldn't even imagine her with anyone else. The very thought repelled me and had me brooding.

After about two hours, she finally opened her eyes and stretched on the bed, looking around. When she saw me on the chair, her face instantly lit up.

"What are you doing?" she asked, sitting up on her elbow. The sheets fell to her waist, revealing to me her magnificent breasts with perky nipples. My cock rose to attention right away.

"Watching you and before that, I was doing some work," I said.

"Where am I?" she asked.

"My office, princess."

Batting her eyelashes, she pulled the sheets aside, showing me the rest of her naked, voluptuous bounty. "You said you're done with work, Daddy?"

Daddy.

Fuck—that pervy shit worked like magic for my

cock. I was rock hard and I wanted to punish her again.

I stood and pulled down my jogging pants, making sure she could see my fully exposed erection as I'd gone commando. I grabbed her chin and made her look at me.

"You're a naughty little brat, you know that? Who the fuck falls asleep in a sex club, alone with a man they just met?" I growled, slipping my hand down to her throat. She had a very beautiful neck, long and graceful, and I bet her pussy was already dripping wet for me.

She swallowed hard, her gaze boring into mine.

"You just wore me out and I couldn't help it. What if I say I am sorry, Daddy?" she cooed, then reached out to caress my bulge.

"You can make it up to me..." Of course I wanted to fuck her again.

Her jaw looked a little red and it was probably because I'd been rough with her. I'd fucked her mouth until she cried, her tears smearing her beautiful face, but she was obedient enough to swallow me without a single word of complaint. That was impressive.

I shut my eyes and let go of her, feeling horny again.

"Let's get you all clean up and then you can go

home," I told her, taking her hand and helping her to get off the bed. I stopped by the door and looked up, seeing that we were standing above the mistletoe. She was still naked, her nipples all perky and pink, ready to be sucked on.

"Oh," she said when she followed my gaze.

Bending down, I took what she offered, devouring her mouth and tasting her all over again. Deep and slow. Her breasts pressed into my chest. I set the pace of the kiss and shifted, making her tilt her head back. When I parted my lips, she followed suit. The feel of her tongue against mine sent a hot, sharp spark of electricity coursing through my veins. The kiss was hot and intense, yet wet and warm and all things nice. Her tongue tangled with mine in a dance as old as time.

Dipping my hand into her lush hair, I savored her. She fit perfectly against my body, tall and curvy and soft. I bit on her lower lip and a moan escaped her mouth.

"Fuck, princess, why do you have to be so perfect?" I ran my hand over her tits, then I bent farther and planted a peck on her right one, followed by small kisses all over her chest. Then, I cupped her breast and sucked on her nipples.

"Ahh..." she sighed.

"Let's take that off, shall we?" she said, grabbing my t-shirt and quickly pulling it over my head.

I dragged her into the bathroom and turned on the shower, then she tugged on my pants. She couldn't undress me fast enough.

"How come you have a bathroom in your office?" she asked, regarding me with lust in her eyes when I was standing naked in front of her.

"Because I sleep in here sometimes when I have shit to do and I like to be fresh when I'm greeting important clients downstairs. Now get in that shower, princess," I ordered her, and before she walked in, I slapped her ass, leaving a red mark there. I could see myself marking her body all over, so she would know she belonged to me.

She went under the surge of water and started washing herself. Luckily, the cubicle was big enough for both of us. Not one to waste time, I dipped my fingers into her folds, quickly discovering she was ready for me.

"And you thought there was a problem with you? That you were frigid?" I said with a chuckle.

She responded by placing her palms against the tile and leaning into it, moaning and panting.

"That's right... That's how you do it," I urged.

"Ivo..."

Her moans fueled me further.

"Is my princess already wet for Daddy? Do you want a hard, stiff cock inside you?" I asked, working my fingers into her cunt.

Swiveling on her feet, she turned around and let her hands explore my chest, tilting her head backwards as I rubbed my cock against her thighs.

"Yes, Daddy," she breathed out as I started to massage her clit. When I strummed her like a violin, I slid my arms under her ass and hefted her up, so I could fuck her against the shower wall. Right away, I rammed my cock into her.

She cried out, eyes closed tight, her tits bouncing in my face as she adjusted her legs around my hips.

"Christ, you're going to give me a heart attack at some point," I grunted, burying my face in her neck. She felt so fucking good, so moist. I started to move in a slow and steady rhythm, while I kissed her everywhere.

"Just keep going and don't you fucking dare stop," she said in a tone that brooked no argument.

"Fucking brat," I muttered before picking up the pace, getting deeper into her core. I couldn't fucking go slow with her—this wasn't my style. Yet, I really wanted to prolong the pleasure. She took all of me in, the water pourin down on us intensifying the sensations.

I sucked on her nipples and fucked her hard,

pumping into her until my heart thumped so loud, it rang in my ears.

"Daddy, *Daddy*! I think I'm going to come!" she cried, arching her body, head thrown back in sheer abandon.

"Good, but before you do, tell your Daddy who you belong to. Tell me that you're mine." I needed to hear it. I needed to feel it. To believe it.

Her flushed face and pink lips swollen from my kisses gave me life. She opened her eyes as I slowed down and we stared at each other for a moment. Time stood still. I didn't know what had gotten into me, but I wanted her to tell me that I owned her. Lock, stock, and motherfucking barrel.

"I'm yours. Daddy, I'm all yours," she finally whispered, her tone laced with emotion.

Oh, I was in so much trouble. How did shit hit the fan so fast?

"That's right, because no one else will ever make you come like I do," I snapped, and I drilled into her harder, faster, deeper until she was screaming for me, pushing her back against the wall. "Yes ... come for me nor. Over ... and over ... and over." She trembled uncontrollably and surrendered to the release.

My own release was near as she came apart over my cock.

It was the most satisfying thing to watch, her

parted lips and her tongue sticking out, licking the corners.

Soon, I ejaculated inside her, catching her lips in a passionate kiss. It took me a moment to pull myself together and when I glanced at my princess, there was a lazy smile on her face.

I was the one who put it there.

"You learn fast," I said. "Let me wash you."

As we showered for real this time, dark thoughts snuck insidiously back to the forefront of my mind.

All of this couldn't have happened at a worst time. For I was either taken, a bargaining chip for Anika's family, or I was a dead man.

I'd be done for, and I wasn't about to go down for anyone.

Pushing the thought out of my head, I focused on the present. I reminded myself to put my Santa hat back on because the spirit of the season had certainly touched me—at least for tonight—jolly as can be. Merry was a helluva present. She'd made me forget all about my stone-cold reality for a while.

Jingle bells.

It was a real shame I had to let her go.

Chapter Seven
LET IT SNOW

Merry

This was fucked up. I hadn't wanted to fall asleep, but Ivo exhausted me so with his sexual energy and charisma, and then I just drifted off, forgetting for a time where I even was. The long nap had been just what I needed, and when I woke up, he was staring at me from the other side of the room.

I never thought I could experience this kind of sex with a man twice my age. It was wild, adventurous, filthy and so kinky. And now he was fucking washing my hair, cleaning my body like this was perfectly acceptable and normal. What was happening to me?

We both knew we weren't going to see each other again. I had commitments to honor. A duty to uphold. My stepmother would make sure of that. But for this one time, this one night, I was able to dream.

So I would be forever thankful to this man, Ivo, for that fantasy he made reality.

I just realized I didn't know his last name. Maybe I shouldn't ask him. It was better this way. Still, I couldn't get rid of the sadness that slowly ate at me.

Ivo was surprisingly gentle when he was washing my hair, massaging my scalp. After that, I returned the favor, squeezing shower gel into my palm, gliding my hands over his body, teasing his cock until he told me to get the fuck out of the stall.

Ivo dried me with a fluffy towel and then found some clothes I could wear. I had his t-shirt and a pair of jeans Candy had left lying around, which would do for my ride home. My dress was ruined, but he assured me he'd replace it.

It didn't matter, really. When we were ready, it was time to say goodbye. The fun was over and I, Merry, needed to face reality once again.

"You know we can't see each other again," I said

when we headed downstairs. I let him know before he said it. Somehow, it felt easier to deal with coming from me. I didn't know what I'd do if the statement had come from him, so I had to preempt it. Ivo glanced at me, pinching his eyebrows together and working his jaw. His silver hair gleamed in the bright light. *Beautiful*.

"This was an amazing experience, but all good things must come to an end. I need to go back."

"Just like that, huh?" he said. A muscle twitched in his jaw. He seemed ... angry. High-strung.

"I'll be graduating next year, then maybe leave LA," I lied.

"Hmmm."

An uncomfortable silence ensued.

"Thank you for everything," I finally said, feeling awkward. "I need to call a cab."

"I'll handle that for you." Getting on the phone, he called somebody by the name of Pete and asked him to come over to pick me up.

"Is that—"

"The guy your friend was fucking last night. I trust him," he said.

I hoped my stepmother was still out of the house, because I really wasn't in the mood to explain myself to her. I normally liked to stay in my dorm room with Tasha, but my stepmother insisted I always stay at the villa on weekends and around the holidays.

Ivo walked me outside. He looked much scarier out in the open air, his dark t-shirt hugging his solid frame, and his jaw rigid. He also looked a little older. My heart was beating dangerously fast as we waited for the taxi.

"You were incredible, Mr. Santa," I said, although he wasn't wearing the hat anymore. I tried to keep my tone cheerful but failed dismally.

"So were you, my little volcano." We stared at each other for a long while. I shivered.

Taking off his jacket, he put it over my shoulders. "Here."

His expression was unreadable, but something flashed in his eyes for the briefest of moments, telling me he wasn't happy about letting me go.

I smiled at him, knowing that soon, he'd turn around and he'd become just another memory.

When a pair of headlights could be seen approaching in the distance, Ivo stepped toward me, up close and personal. The look in his eyes right then was one that rooted me to the spot. He seemed so different. Unapproachable.

A cold shiver ran up my spine. He was clearly wrestling with some demons, and there was nothing I could do to fix this.

"What—"

"Let me tell you something, princess. Sometimes,

we get more than we bargained for." He caressed my cheek with the back of his hand, a fleeting touch. His expression softened. "So never say never."

And with that, he stepped back and waited until I was bundled up in the car, then walked away from me,back inside.

As Pete drove away from the curb in front of the club, remaining blessedly silent, tears started falling down and my heart broke for I knew that was the last I'd see of my Daddy.

Only then did I realize: I was still wearing his jacket, which smelled of cinnamon and Scotch with a hint of smoke.

A few weeks later

"Oh, come on, we have to get back there. Pete was incredible," Tasha whinged into the phone, and I couldn't help rolling my eyes.

"I told you, I don't want to. It was a one time thing for me. It was wonderful, and I don't regret any of it, but we are not going back there ever again. At least I'm not," I said in a firm tone. I opened my text book, trying to focus on studying for my exam.

Not on orgasms with hot men with silver-streaked hair

"Gee, you're no fun," she said before hanging up.

She was right. I was no longer having fun. The last couple of weeks had been very stressful. Next year I would be graduating, so I had a lot on my plate. My visit to the sex club had definitely helped teach me about myself. I finally knew that I wasn't a freak of nature and was capable of having an orgasm.

Many orgasms.

But now I had to put my nose to the grindstone and think about my future. Also, I had to stop thinking about Ivo and how he'd made me feel. He was a guy with only a first name, and would always be such to me. An incredible, handsome, delightfully domineering and kinky man who'd given me sex that exceeded all my expectations.

The holiday season seemed strange this year, because every time I noticed certain decorations, I kept thinking about Ivo and the club and then of course about all the kinky stuff he did to me.

I'd also met his two sons, who'd failed to give me what I'd gone there for. The thought of what I'd done made me blush even now, weeks later. I couldn't wrap my mind around the fact I'd fucked a father and his two sons in one night. Wow, that was a mouthful—in more ways than one.

My stepmother must have noticed how distracted I'd been, because she kept asking what was wrong. I didn't know what to say to her, so I did my best to avoid her.

With a sigh, I forced my attention to my book.

Sometime later, I heard a doorbell ring and slammed the heavy tome on the desk, hoping I wouldn't have to get up and see who it was. *Always something or someone interrupting my concentration.* I had a crapload of stuff to do and I knew my sister was bored out of her mind, so she could deal with whoever was at the door.

Five minutes later, I heard Clara's footsteps and then she opened the door to my room. She looked flushed, as if she'd run all the way here.

"What is it?" I asked.

"There is someone downstairs asking for you," she said, and before I could ask her who it was, she vanished.

I shook my head in irritation and stormed out of my room. After my father's death, my stepmother made us all live in this mansion—until I went to college and insisted on experiencing how everybody else lived. However, she'd already told me that if I wanted to keep studying next year, I'd have to move out of the dorm and stay home. The whole house was just too big for us and it was no use if we didn't have at least a housekeeper who could answer the fucking door, like any other normal crime boss family.

I laughed at that thought. 'Normal' and 'crime boss' did not go together in a sentence. I sounded like a spoiled brat reasoning this way, but it was the truth.

I walked into the living room, where a man waited. He had his back to me and he was wearing a tailored suit. He looked quite distinguished.

A spark of awareness trilled through me.

"May I help you?" I asked, and when he turned around, my legs nearly gave out on me.

Ivo.

He was in my house, standing in my living room, looking absolutely breathtaking—exactly the same as I remembered. Tall, dark, with that glimmer in his eyes that slowly turned me into a pile of goo.

"Hello, princess. Daddy missed you."

Thank you for reading! We appreciate you.
If you enjoyed this book,
the next in the series, Her Surrender (Men of Sin
Book one), is available on pre-order today. Click here
to get it now!
Also, please consider joining our lists to get notified
of all our hot new releases (promise we don't spam!):
Josie Marks
Mina Snowe

Her Surrender (Men of Sin Book 1)

Amazon US
Amazon UK
Amazon AUS
Amazon CA